EX LIBRIS
THIS BOOK BELONGS TO

VOLUME TWO

ROMAN MYTHS

FIONA MACDONALD

SCRIBBLERS

a SALARIYA *imprint*

Published in Great Britain in MMXX by
Scribblers, an imprint of
The Salariya Book Company Ltd
25 Marlborough Place,
Brighton BN1 1UB
www.salariya.com

© The Salariya Book Company Ltd
MMXX

HB ISBN-13: 978-1-912904-83-9

3 5 7 9 8 6 4 2 1

A CIP catalogue record for this book
is available from the British Library.

Printed and bound in China.

Illustrations by:

Patrick Brooks
Sun, Moon and Stars
Always Welcome
Kidnapped!
Hooray For Heroes
The Geese That Saved Rome

Serena Lombardo
The Water Spirit Who Talked Too Much
Two Wonderful Women and A
Wicked One
Past, Present, Future

Visit
www.salariya.com
for our online catalogue and
free fun stuff.

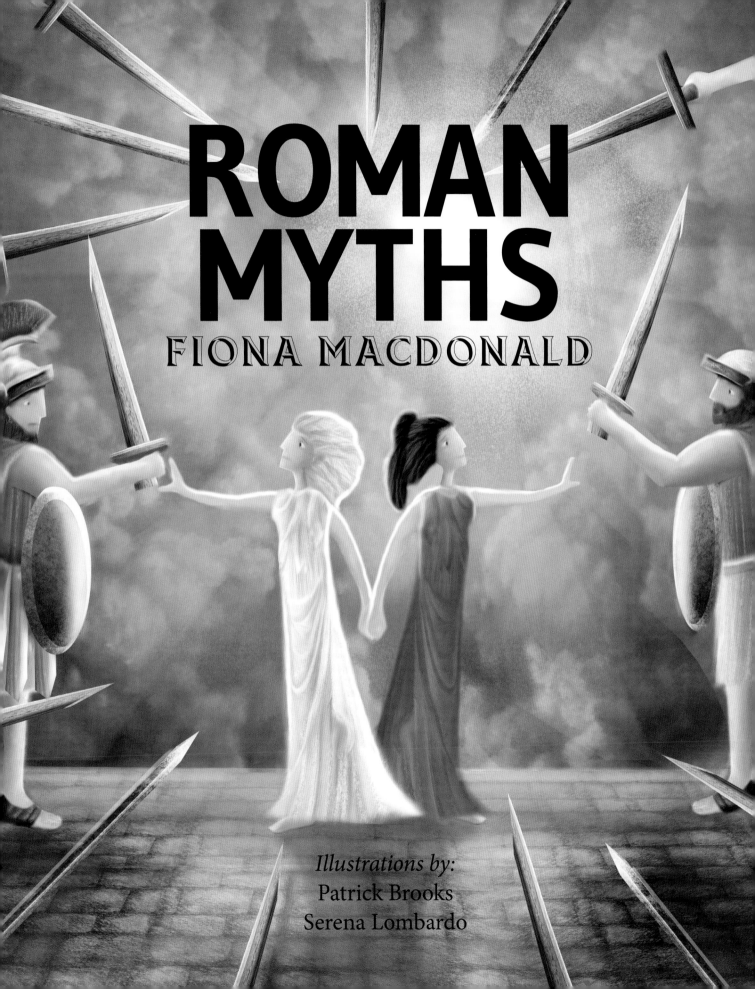

ROMAN
MYTHS

FIONA MACDONALD

Illustrations by:

Patrick Brooks

Serena Lombardo

CONTENTS

INTRODUCTION

This book recounts some of the best-known myths and legends from Ancient Rome. They have all been enjoyed for over 2,000 years. When you read them, you'll be entering into the thoughts and hopes and fears and dreams of people who lived when Rome was a great city, with fantastic temples and palaces, when Roman engineers devised great new inventions, and when Roman army legions patrolled the frontiers of an empire that stretched from Scotland to Syria.

Reading myths from any past civilisation, including Rome and its empire, is like time-travel for the mind. We can see and touch the remains of buildings and earthworks that the Romans left behind; myths and legends help us learn what those Roman builders, and their parents and wives and slaves and children, were thinking.

Why do we and other peoples tell stories? For all sorts of reasons. Myths and legends (traditional tales that may or may not be true) are the world's oldest tales. They have survived because they are entertaining, funny, scary, inspiring and sad. But much more than that: myths and legends carry a message. They are stories with a meaning. They helped people in the past, and may still help us today, to make sense of the world.

Roman myths and legends also tell the story of a particular group of people: refugees from a glorious city destroyed by war. They describe the heroism of the survivors, and how they fought against all kinds of dangers to find a new place to settle. There, they created a wonderful new civilisation. It still shapes our language and literature. We can still admire it today.

SUN, MOON AND STARS

She was beautiful, they said. Beautiful and deadly. Diana, goddess of hunting, the wild woods and the silvery Moon. She was tall, proud, brave, strong and fierce as a lion. She raced through the forests with her pack of hunting dogs, blood dripping from their jaws. She rode a flying chariot pulled by fleet-footed deer. She turned people into animals; wild beasts obeyed her. Priests offered her human sacrifices. And little girls dressed up as bears to dance in her honour. She was shining, cold and pitiless, like the Moon.

Like the Moon, too, Diana was alone. Her only companions were her brother, Apollo the Sun-god, strange, shy forest nymphs and young, unmarried girls. No man, not even a god, dared love her. And she vowed not to love any man. Until, until…

Endymion was a shepherd, and very, very handsome. In summer, he led his flocks high into the mountains. All day, he worked hard. At night, tired after all his efforts, he stretched out on soft grass on the mountain top, closed his eyes and fell into a deep, dreamless sleep.

High overhead, shining in the night sky, Diana saw Endymion. How could any ordinary man be so good-looking? Every night, she came closer, closer, closer to gaze at him as he lay sleeping. She said nothing, he heard nothing (the Moon is silent) but, just perhaps, she might have given him a sweet, gentle kiss from time to time.

Nothing is secret from Jupiter, king of the gods. He saw Diana with Endymion and he was not pleased. Should he punish Endymion with death, like any other man who caught sight of Diana, even accidentally? No! Diana had chosen to fall in love with Endymion; the shepherd was not guilty. Jupiter decided: he would give Endymion a gift. But it was a perilous one, with a terrible price to pay, like most favours from gods to humans. Jupiter would let Endymion live forever, so long as he stayed asleep all the time.

Orion was a giant, and a mighty hunter. Not quite a human, not quite a god, not quite a monster, he was tough but good-hearted. So Jupiter allowed him to spend time with Diana and her wild beasts in the forests, because the two of them shared a passionate love for hunting.

Diana was a brilliant huntress, of course, and no man on earth was as good as Orion. The two soon became inseparable. They practised shooting with bows and arrows or hurling spears at targets. They tracked the footprints of wolves and wild boar; they trained young hunting-dogs together. They were good friends, like brother and sister.

Diana's real brother, her twin, Apollo the Sun-god, grew very, very jealous. How dare Orion spend so much time with his sister? And what if Diana should one day fall in love with Orion? Apollo shuddered at the thought. 'And remember', he said to himself, 'Jupiter has ordered Diana not to marry. Everyone – even a giant – must obey his laws. It's time to take action!'

It was early one bright autumn morning, which is the best time for hunting, when Apollo appeared suddenly, as if by magic, in a little clearing in the forest. Diana was already there with a few of her best dogs, waiting for Orion. The grass was still wet with dew and little wisps of mist still hung around the trees and bushes. A few slanting rays of sunlight shone through the branches, surrounding Apollo with a golden glow.

'Good morning, sister!' said Apollo, smiling very pleasantly. 'A great day for hunting! Is that a new bow you've got there? A gift from Orion, perhaps? Can I see?'

He stretched out his hand, and Diana handed the bow over. Yes, it was new. And yes, it had been a present. One of the best she'd ever had. Apollo examined it closely, and then frowned just a little.

'Hmmm…' he said, thoughtfully. 'It certainly looks good. But what's it like in action?'

He looked up and gazed around the clearing. Then he pointed at a shadowy shape in the mist, just beyond the bushes.

'See that, over there?' he said, pointing to the shadow. 'Looks like a stag to me. Could an arrow from your new bow hit it, moving?'

Apollo clapped his hands, and the misty shape began to move away.

Diana didn't stop to think. She grabbed the bow from her brother's hand, chose one of her sharpest arrows and sent it flying through the air.

The shape gave a cry of agony and slumped on the forest floor.

'Good shot!' said Apollo. 'Well done!'

He frowned again, and continued. 'Strange how deer can sometimes sound almost human...'

Diana went pale. Pale as the new Moon in a cloudy sky. She flung her bow to the ground and rushed towards the shadowy shape. It was no longer moving.

She crouched down and turned the shape over. It was Orion. Dead with an arrow through his heart.

Diana could not bring Orion back to life on Earth. But she could do the next best thing. She carried him and his hunting dogs up into the heavens and turned them into constellations: brightly-shining

patterns of stars. That way, Orion could still be her companion. They could stride across the skies and race through the clouds together, as once they had hunted side by side in her lovely forests. Every night. For ever and ever.

THE WATER SPIRIT WHO TALKED TOO MUCH

The god of the River Almo had a daughter, the water spirit Lara. A lively, friendly girl, she was always chattering or laughing. Her babble never stopped but flowed on, night and day, just like the river waters that were her home.

'Bubbly' was one way to describe Lara. 'A nuisance' was another. She made so much noise that 'La-La' would have been a better name for her, or even 'La-La-La-La-La'!

17

'Hush, child,' said her father, covering his ears with hands dripping wet with river-water. 'Shh! Shh! Please stop talking.' But Lara chattered on.

Even worse, Lara was a terrible gossip. She could never keep a secret. She was always whispering and giggling with the other water spirits as they sat on the river bank making garlands of wild flowers, or combing river-weed out of their lovely long hair.

But then, one day, Lara found out that Jupiter, king of the gods, was becoming friendly with her sister.

'He's her new boyfriend!' Lara cried, while the water spirits gasped in horror. 'I've been watching them,' she said.

'Tell us! Tell us!' cried the other water spirits. But Lara shook her head.

'No! I'm not telling you anything more. But...'

She jumped up and down in the water.

'But I'm going to tell Jupiter's wife, Queen Juno. She might give me a reward!'

Juno was famously proud and even more famously jealous. She flew into a rage when she heard what Lara had to say. (And she didn't reward Lara. Instead, she shouted at her to go away.)

Jupiter was absolutely furious. He vowed to punish Lara. He thought long and hard: what would be the best way to take his revenge?

At last, Jupiter decided. He froze Lara's tongue so that she could no longer talk or tell any more secrets. Then he commanded his son, the messenger-god Mercury, to take Lara to the Underworld, to live in a place that was cold, dark and silent. As silent as a tomb.

It one was of Mercury's many jobs to lead dead souls to the Underworld, and so he knew the way.

THE WATER SPIRIT WHO TALKED TOO MUCH

Their path ran through a secret wood, a beautiful place with the last, fading rays of sunlight and sweet-smelling flowers.

'Let's rest here a while,' said Mercury, giving Lara a comforting hug and a friendly smile.

'Let's enjoy the land of the living for just a little longer, before we head underground.'

Lara nodded, silently, and, for the first time, stopped crying. She liked Mercury. He was kind and funny and charming. She wanted to stay with him in the secret wood forever.

One thing led to another, and Lara became the mother of twins.

But Jupiter's commands cannot be ignored. Mercury led Lara, now weeping again, away from the sunlight and down, down, down into the dark and the silence. But although Lara's life on earth was over, she lived on in the Underworld. Some say she was given a new name, Tacita (The Silent One) and that she ruled over a kingdom of dead souls. No longer a silly, chattering girl, she became a queen, respected and feared by all.

Lara's twins stayed in the land of the living, and, as children of the god Mercury, were themselves honoured as gods. Like Lara, the twins were speechless and silent. And they were named after her: the Lares.

Many, many years later, Roman men, women and children worshipped the Lares at a little shrine inside each family home. They thought of the Lares as the spirits of dead ancestors, who guarded and protected living family members.

Lara's life on Earth was short, but her fame lived on and she, and her children, stayed powerful. As the Romans said, the gods never die.

ALWAYS WELCOME

Always active, always questioning, always on the move, Mercury wore magic boots and a hat with wings to help him speed round the world. He was the god of messages and messengers, good news and bad, travellers and traders, ventures and adventures.

Once upon a time, Mercury and his father Jupiter, king of the gods, set off on a summertime journey. They disguised themselves as ordinary travellers: an old man and a lively young lad. That way, they could meet and talk to ordinary men and women.

The two gods' voices, normally so rich and strong, became rough and rather feeble. Their fine robes were replaced by old and scruffy clothes. Jupiter and Mercury took nothing else with them, except a strong stick for walking, and a cloak in case it rained. If they needed anything else, well, they had magic.

It was nearly evening when the two 'travellers', still in disguise, reached a remote little village in a valley in the mountains. They had tramped all day through wild countryside in the heat and dust of summer. Now they hoped to find water to drink, beds to sleep in and (if they were lucky) some sort of evening meal. Long, long ago, there were no hotels where travellers could stay. Instead, everyone relied on the kindness of strangers.

Tired and hungry, Jupiter and Mercury knocked politely at the first cottage they came to.

'Good evening, Sir', said Jupiter, to the suspicious-looking farmer who opened the door.

'We are travellers, looking for somewhere to stay for the night. Can you perhaps give us shelter, and something to eat? We have money. We can pay...'

The door slammed shut in Jupiter's face, as the farmer shouted, 'No! Get out! We don't want your sort here!'

Jupiter shrugged. 'Unfriendly!' he said. 'Not very nice. Well, let's try this house, here.'

But again and again, the travellers were sent away with angry words. A couple of tough-looking farmhands even threatened to hit them.

'What a terrible place!' said Mercury, with a sigh. 'And what horrible people!'

'What now, lord and father? Shall we spread out our cloaks and sleep on the ground? Or walk on to the next village? But it's getting late and that is several miles away.'

A cool evening breeze stirred the branches of trees growing by the roadside. Jupiter grabbed his son Mercury's shoulder, and pointed. 'Look!' he said. 'Look over there!'

A faint light glowed and flickered, half hidden by the branches.

'It's a little tumbledown cottage!' said Mercury, grinning with excitement. 'The last house in the village! Let's try there!'

Meanwhile, in the neat garden surrounding the cottage, old Philemon stopped weeding his vegetables, stood up straight, rubbed his aching back (Ah! that felt better...) and walked slowly towards the door. A welcoming light from an oil lamp shone out into the dusk. To his great surprise, Philemon saw a couple of strangers standing there.

He stopped, and wiped his grimy hands on his earth-stained tunic.

'Good evening,' he said. 'Welcome, I'm sure! This is a surprise! We weren't expecting visitors, but you'll step inside, surely, and rest a while by our warm fire.'

He walked a little way to one side and called through the cottage doorway. 'Baucis, my dear! We have guests!'

Then he turned to the dusty 'travellers'. 'Now, sir. Now, young fellow. This way! Follow me!'

Relieved, smiling, grateful, Jupiter and Mercury sat by the fire. A thin, older woman with a careworn but kindly face bustled about, adding twigs to the fire, bringing rough wool blankets and straw cushions to make their wooden seats more comfortable. This was Baucis, Philemon's wife. Together they lived here at the top of the valley: growing their own food, rearing their own animals and (just about) managing to keep their old and crumbling cottage in repair.

Carefully, Philemon poured refreshing drinks of rough wine, mixed with cool, sweet spring water.

Next, Philemon entertained his visitors with cheerful stories and friendly questions – where had they come from? where were they going? – while Baucis brought out all the food she had in her larder to offer to her guests. It was simple, but it was a feast! There were shining black olives, fresh green salad leaves, crunchy radishes and turnips, eggs and a lump of sour-milk cheese. For dessert, Baucis offered her visitors nuts, berries, dried figs and prunes ('All from our garden! I picked them myself!'), together with fresh grapes and apples. Jupiter and Mercury enjoyed it all. Everything was delicious!

'Squaaawwk! Squaawwk!' Suddenly, the meal was interrupted by a flurry of wings. Baucis had caught hold of her last surviving goose; it had wandered into the kitchen. She clasped it to her tightly, stroking its soft feathers and looking rather wistful.

'Shall I kill and cook it for you sirs?' she said. 'Roast goose is very good eating...'

Jupiter leaped to his feet, almost knocking over his chair and the table. 'No! Never! Let it live!' he said. 'Baucis and Philemon, you have been more than generous. No king or god could do more. Even I...' he paused, trying not to reveal that he was not an ordinary traveller. He began again...

'No right-thinking person would want you to do that! Let the creature enjoy life here, in your wonderful garden.'

He turned to Philemon. 'But, my friend, if you're offering, I wouldn't say no to another bowl of your good wine and water.'

Baucis left, to shut the goose away safely in its pen. The men sat together round the dying fire. Mysteriously, the little jug of wine, which was all Philemon had, never seemed to grow empty. The talk flowed; there were jokes and laughter.

Philemon lived a simple life, but he was not stupid. Slowly, he began to wonder, were these travellers all that they seemed? He'd never met anyone like them before. He began to be afraid. Baucis came indoors and sat down beside her husband, quietly reaching out under the table to hold his hand.

Mercury was quick and subtle. Jupiter was wise. They understood how the old couple were feeling. Jupiter raised his hand. There was a flash, like lightning, and a rumble, like thunder. Philemon and Baucis clasped each other tightly.

'Good friends!' the gods said together. 'Please don't be afraid. Yes, we are gods in disguise. But we want to honour you, not harm you. Unlike everyone else in your village, you have welcomed us, shared all you have with us and treated us with respect and kindness. Now we wish to reward you! Would you like gold, or a new cottage, or hundreds of geese?'

Shyly, Philemon stood up. He coughed and glanced at Baucis.

'Good sirs,' he said. 'We thank you from the

bottom of our hearts. But truly, all I want, and my wife feels the same, is for us to go on living happily here together. And then, if you can please arrange it, ahem...'

He coughed again.

'It's like this. We both want to die at the same time! We've been in love since we were teenagers, and we wouldn't want to go on living if we couldn't be together.

'If you really want to repay us for our help – and it was nothing special; we'd do the same for any travellers – then please, please let Baucis and me die at the same time, side by side.'

'Philemon, you have my promise!' said Jupiter, looking suddenly very serious. He raised his hand again, and nodded his mighty head.

The world went dark. Philemon and Baucis felt themselves spinning round and round. When they woke up, it was pouring with rain and they were on top of a high mountain, looking down to where their village had once been. But it was no longer there. Instead, a deep lake filled the valley. Philemon and Baucis stood speechless, astonished.

Jupiter spoke again. 'Friends, we must soon go on our way. But this is what I command you to do. Build a little temple here in my honour, and live in it, to take care of it, for the rest of your lives.

'The village and the villagers are drowned. It is their punishment. But travellers will come to the temple, and...' Jupiter smiled, and it was like the Sun lighting up the whole sky, 'I know you will welcome them.'

Philemon and Baucis lived on for many, many years. But at last they grew so old and weary that they wanted to rest for ever. Hand in hand, they stood in front of the temple, gazing up at the sky. Jupiter saw them, and kept his promise.

As the world went dark for a final time for Philemon and Baucis, their feet became rooted to the ground, their bodies were clothed in warm brown bark, while leaves and branches sprouted from their fingers.

They say that the two ancient trees still stand outside the temple. Over the centuries, their branches have grown together and can't be parted. Travellers still stop, to marvel at them.

'See, it's Philemon and Baucis. Still in love. Still holding hands.'

KIDNAPPED!

■■■■■■■■■■■■■■■■■■■■■■■■■

The first inhabitants of the city of Rome had a rather peculiar problem: there were not enough women! Rome was founded by a soldier-king and his army. They marked out the streets. They built the walls and gates and houses. They went hunting in the hills and fishing in the river. They bargained for grain and fruit with farmers living nearby. And yes, you've guessed, most of them were men.

And there was one thing that even the strongest, bravest Roman men could not do. They could not have babies.

Without children to grow up after them, the first Romans feared that all their hard work would be wasted. When they grew old and died, there would be no new young Romans to take their places. The city, the community, even the name of Rome might die and be forgotten.

At first, King Romulus tried peaceful invitations. He sent ambassadors to all the surrounding kingdoms, asking them, politely, to send some young women to Rome. There, the women would marry Roman soldiers and become the mothers of Roman babies. Rome would be saved!

We don't know what the young women thought of this idea (though we can perhaps imagine). But in any case, they were going nowhere. All the neighbouring rulers said 'no'. The ambassadors returned to Rome, ashamed and miserable. Their mission had failed.

Once again, the Romans asked themselves, 'What can we do?' Some hot-headed soldiers called for war. They would attack nearby cities, capture the women and carry them back to Rome.

King Romulus was by now very old, but also very wise. 'No!' he said. 'I have a much better plan. Be quiet, and listen!'

It was not long before Roman ambassadors were on the move again. This time, they were heading for the land of the Sabines, the closest kingdom to Rome. And, this time, the ambassadors carried invitations. All the Sabine people, men, women and children, were invited to a splendid sports festival, like the Olympic Games, to be held in Rome.

This time, the Sabines accepted. They thought it would be safe, exciting, and fun. They knew that people travelling to the Olympic Games were protected by the 'Olympic Peace', decreed by the gods. They thought it would be the same in Rome. They looked forward to watching super-fit athletes, rough, tough wrestlers, thrilling chariot races and much more.

It was a trick, of course. A cruel, clever Roman trick. At first all went well. The games were spectacular and a great success! But then, at a secret signal, while the Sabines were happily watching the races in the sunshine, Roman men seized all the young Sabine women, and carried them, kicking and screaming and weeping and wailing, to Roman houses with barred windows and strong doors.

After that, and this was just as shameful, they chased all the Sabine mothers and fathers, brothers and little sisters back across the border. Of course, the Sabines were outraged, disgusted, horrified! But, surrounded by Roman soldiers, they were also powerless.

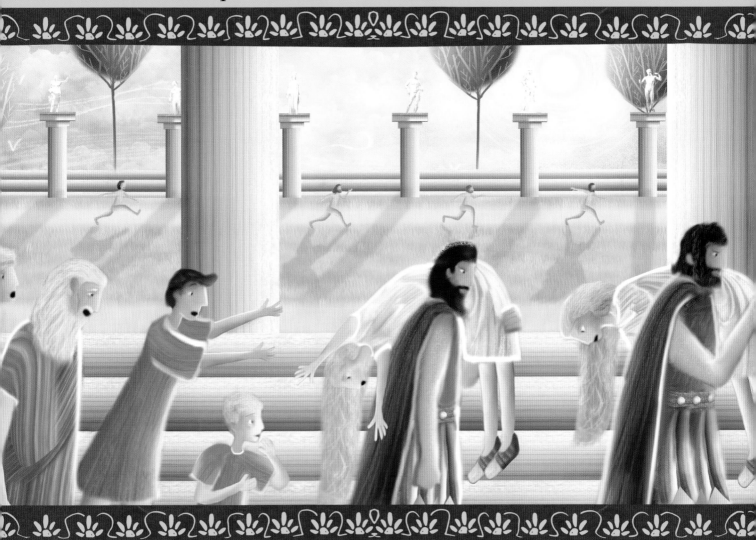

Soon after, the Sabines came back with a mighty army, swearing to take revenge on the Roman kidnappers and to bring their daughters back home. Sabine soldiers smashed their way into the

city and began to slaughter all the Romans they could find. But this bloodshed was simply too much for the Sabine women to bear. Bravely, they rushed out of the Roman houses where they were now living and flung themselves into the middle of the fighting.

'Stop!' they yelled. 'Stop at once! Drop those swords! Throw away those spears. We mean it! DO IT NOW!

'We were brought here by violence, and we have seen how much suffering that violence has caused our families. We don't want any more killing, any more pain, any more grief and loss.

'We women, Sabines by birth, Romans by marriage, were kidnapped on purpose, to bring new life to Rome. But all you men want is death. Death and destruction.

'If you value us, if you need us, if you love us, STOP FIGHTING. Let us all live in peace!'

HOORAY
FOR
HEROES

The Romans were proud of their past. And they loved myths and legends about brave Roman heroes who had lived long ago. Were these stories true? Did the events they describe actually happen? Perhaps not. But the stories were still important, because they taught Roman citizens the proper 'Roman' way to behave. Here are a few favourite Roman hero stories, about Horatius, about Mucius and about three brave brothers:

44

HORATIUS AT THE BRIDGE

Rome was in danger. Real, deadly danger. The city was surrounded by formidable armies led by King Lars Porsena of the Etruscans, an ancient people who had lived in Italy long before Rome was built. Already, Etruscan troops had overrun the outskirts of the city. Now they were planning to force their way across the great bridge that spanned the wide River Tiber to reach the heart of the city. If they succeeded, Rome and the Romans would die.

Roman commanders led a desperate attack out of the city, to try to drive the Etruscan armies away. But, for once, the Roman army was not strong enough. The Romans were overpowered. All they could do was retreat.

Romans did not easily give up a fight. But now it seemed to most of them that there was nothing more they could do.

Only Horatius, Roman Captain of the Gate, had other ideas. He was a soldier, it was his duty to fight.

'If I have to die,' he said, 'then I will die bravely, fighting for my homeland, for the spirits of my ancestors and for the Roman gods. A true Roman is not a coward and nor am I!'

Two of his fellow-soldiers, Spurius and Titus, hurried to stand beside him. 'We are true Romans, too!' they cried. 'We will stay here with you! We'll defend the bridge with our lives!'

Next, Horatius turned to face the rabble of Roman soldiers, hurrying across the bridge.

'Run, run for your lives, men!' he yelled. 'And once you're safely on the other side, destroy the bridge behind you. The Etruscans won't be able to get into Rome. Our city will be saved!'

The soldiers did as Horatius commanded. Meanwhile, with Spurius and Titus beside him,

Horatius fought off spears and arrows from the advancing Etruscan army.

At last, just one narrow plank was left from the bridge. The fast-flowing river surged and swirled far below.

'Friends! Comrades!' barked Horatius. 'Save yourselves! Go back to Rome while you can. Our task here is nearly completed. I'll stay and keep the Etruscans away until you've got to the other side.'

'But, but...' Spurius and Titus protested. 'We can't leave you here to die!'

'No arguments!' shouted Horatius. 'That's an order! Go!'

With a sickening creak and groan, the great bridge finally collapsed. As the timbers swayed and cracked beneath his feet, Horatius was thrown into the river. Etruscan soldiers, who had nearly reached him now, hurled a hail of spears, while floating wreckage from the bridge battered him from all sides.

Some say the goddess Roma helped. Others say that Horatius was simply a strong swimmer. But however it happened, Horatius survived. Panting and gasping, he struggled ashore, safely back in Rome, while Etruscan soldiers stood baffled and helpless on the other side.

'LEFTY': HERO OR VICTIM?

It's a bold story, a brave story, but also a tragic one. Gaius Mucius joined the Roman army, like Horatius, at the time when Etruscan armies were camped, ready to attack, in fields all around Rome. Strong, a fast runner and quick-witted, he was popular with his fellow soldiers. Soon, he was spotted by army commanders.

'That new recruit looks promising!' said one. 'The ideal man for the Senate's secret mission.'

'Are you sure?' replied his comrade. 'He's very young, and he's very likely to get killed. Can we spare good soldiers like him?'

They talked on, and eventually agreed that young Mucius should be entrusted with the task. But what was it? What were his orders? Murder! The Senate, the ruling council of Rome, had decided that the best way to defeat the Etruscans would be to get rid of their king, Lars Porsena. So Mucius was, as we might say today, 'licensed to kill'.

Very early one morning, Mucius left Rome, sped across the fields and found his way secretly into the Etruscan camp. It was the soldiers' pay day, and already there were groups of men waiting to receive their wages. There was also a wooden platform with two folding chairs. One was where the king would sit; the other was for a scribe. Mucius hid in the shadow of a nearby tent and waited there.

A sudden fanfare of blaring trumpets made him

jump. The soldiers sprang to attention, and a tall, commanding-looking man strode into the room. He wore a magnificent cloak. So did the royal paymaster who walked respectfully behind him, followed by soldiers carrying wooden chests filled with coins.

Mucius tensed himself, ready to attack. He let the first few Etruscans pass by, smiling and pleased with their wages, and then, when the king and the paymaster put their heads together to discuss, so it seemed, some sort of problem, Mucius dashed out from the shadows, leaped on to the wooden platform and stabbed, stabbed, stabbed with his short, sharp sword.

At first, there was chaos, but soon Mucius felt his sword knocked from his grip, rough hands twisting his arms behind his back and the tip of a sharp dagger pressed against his throat. Angry, excited voices cursed him in Etruscan. He did not understand the words, but he could guess what they were saying.

Carefully, because that dagger was dangerously close, Mucius raised his head slightly and tried to look around. He could see one body, still wearing its cloak, bleeding to death on the floor. For a moment, he felt a surge of triumph. His mission had succeeded!

But who was this, walking towards him, surrounded by scowling bodyguards? By Jupiter! It was the king, Lars Porsena himself. Shaken, but very much alive, and very, very angry.

Mucius had killed the paymaster.

'Who is this hateful enemy, this spy, this murderer?' snarled the king.

Mucius did not wait for anyone else to answer. 'I am a Roman citizen,' he cried. 'I came here ready to kill, but I'm also ready to die.'

'And, believe me,' he continued, 'Back in Rome, there are three hundred more soldiers all keen and willing to do the same as me. We Romans don't care what pain or danger we suffer. Just look...'

And before anyone could stop him, Mucius darted across to the fire that had been burning to keep the king and the paymaster warm. He thrust his right hand into the flames and held it there until the flesh burned away.

'Ye gods, boy!' exclaimed Lars Porsena. 'You're a greater danger to yourself than ever you were to me! But you're brave, very brave. I admire that.'

And he let Mucius go free.

Back in Rome, Mucius was praised and rewarded. He was given the nickname Scaevolus ('Lefty'), and it was used as a proud surname by his descendants for centuries.

Because of his reckless self-sacrifice, Mucius escaped death. But he spent the rest of his life with a useless right arm, in pain for most of the time.

BRAVE BROTHERS

Long before Horatius defended the great bridge at Rome, three Roman brothers, who shared his name, also won praise as warriors, who fought so that the rest of the Roman people would not have to go to war.

From its very beginning, Rome had to battle against neighbouring cities and kingdoms. The Romans were newcomers. They had settled on other peoples' land. They believed that their gods gave them a right to do this, but their neighbours did not always agree.

One thing that Rome and many rival cities did agree on, however, was that war wasted money and destroyed innocent lives. And so, when the leaders of Rome and the city of Alba Longa found themselves threatening to fight, they had the good sense to say 'Stop! Let's think! Let's talk!'

It was the king of Alba Longa who came up with the plan. 'We both have strong, brave soldiers,' he said. 'Why don't we ask just a few of them to fight a duel? That will settle the argument between us, and only a few soldiers will be killed.'

The Romans agreed. But who would be their champions? By a strange coincidence, the Romans and the people of Alba Longa both counted teams of three brothers among their best fighting men.

'Let them fight for us!' both sides agreed. The Roman brothers were known as the Horatii. Raising their swords high, in honour of the gods, they swore a solemn oath to defend Rome.

It was a grim day. Death hung in the air. On each side, the champions flexed their muscles, tried on their battle-armour, said prayers, made sacrifices to the gods and prepared to fight each other to the bitter end.

'Tonight, we might meet in the Underworld,' said the Horatii to each other. 'Brothers, whatever happens, in life or death, we will not be divided.'

Then they stepped out on to the battlefield, where the men from Alba Longa were waiting for them.

Both sides fought bravely. As the battle raged on, everyone could see that all three Alba Longa brothers were seriously wounded, and two Horatii had been killed. Only one, whose name was Publius, was left standing. Did this mean defeat for Rome?

For a while, that seemed certain. But Publius would not give in. He ran away, zig-zagging all over the battlefield. It was a trick, and it worked! His opponents did not know which way to turn. Instead of fighting side by side, guarding each other, they split up and became separate targets. One by one, Publius speared them all.

Yes, it was a brave and clever victory. But it was tragic, at the same time. Five fine young men lay dead. Two proud families mourned. And worse, much worse was to follow.

Long before the battle, Camilla, Publius's sister, had fallen in love with one of the brothers from Alba Longa. She had given him a splendid robe that she had woven herself. But then – oh no, what was this? – she saw Publius dragging the robe behind him. Wild with grief and sorrow, Camilla rushed at her brother.

'You brute!' she cried, 'You've killed him!'

And what did Publius do next? He killed poor Camilla, his own sister.

'She deserved it,' he said. 'She was not loyal to Rome.'

TWO WONDERFUL WOMEN
AND A WICKED ONE

Held captive as a wartime hostage, Cloelia organised a daring escape and then went back to prison again. Why did she do this? To help Rome!

It happened this way. During the long, bitter war between Rome and the Etruscans, both sides agreed to a truce while their leaders tried to make peace. But before talks could begin, the Etruscans demanded hostages: Roman boys and girls.

'We'll keep them to make sure that you don't break your promise,' the Etruscans said. 'Any sign of an attack and these young Romans will die!'

The Etruscans treated the hostages pretty well. They had food, and tents – some for the boys, some for the girls – and blankets. But armed guards kept watch on them day and night.

The hostages were frightened, of course. They knew that they might die. But, almost as bad, they were bored. There was nowhere they could go and nothing they could do. They sat around, growing more and more depressed. The days seemed endless. They missed their families.

'I can't bear this any longer!' said Cloelia. 'I've got to get out of here! It's not that far to the river bank. I could try to swim across... Is anyone coming with me?'

But how could girls get out of a camp full of well-armed soldiers? Cloelia had a plan.

'Come close and listen,' she whispered to the others. 'This is what we'll do…'

It was a peaceful evening. Little groups of soldiers sat around talking with their mates. The night guard marched rather lazily round the tents; they were not expecting an attack.

Suddenly, there was a commotion in the tent where the girls were sitting. A few half-stifled shrieks, followed by whispers and giggling.

'I SAW him!' called one of the girls, pointing into the half-darkness. 'A Roman soldier! Over there! Do you think he's come to rescue us?'

'SHUT UP! SHUT UP!' yelled Cloelia, rushing to put her hand across the other girl's mouth, while the other girls cried 'They'll hear us!'

That, of course, was just what Cloelia planned.

The lazy night patrol and a posse of rather sleepy

bodyguards dashed off to where the girls had just been pointing.

'NOW!' said Cloelia. Quickly, very quietly, she led the girls out of the camp. Then they all raced away, down towards the river. Etruscan soldiers lumbered after them, but the girls were lighter and faster. Following Cloelia, they leapt into the water and swam safely across to Rome.

King Lars Porsena was furious. With Cloelia, of course, but mostly with his own soldiers.

'Stupid fools!' he shouted. 'You've been tricked!'

The king knew that he would look foolish, too. He must win back some respect.

'The best way to do that,' he said to himself, 'is to show that I can behave more honourably than the Romans. By running away, Cloelia has broken the rules of the truce. I could, maybe I should, kill the hostages that I still have here, then attack and destroy Rome.'

'But I'll show those Romans who's the better man! I'll offer to continue the truce, BUT only if that wretched Cloelia agrees to come back here.'

Fighting back the tears, Cloelia said farewell to her parents and was marched away by some surly Etruscan guards.

They led her to where King Lars Porsena was sitting in his tent.

'You did a silly thing when you ran away,' he said. 'And a dishonourable one. But even so, you were very brave, and you're being brave now by coming back as a hostage. I admire that, so I won't kill you. In fact, I'll set you free.'

'And,' he continued, 'I'll prove that Etruscans can be generous and merciful. You can take some more Roman hostages back to your city with you.'

He turned to the guards. 'Take her away, men,' he commanded. 'And tell the Roman leaders that the truce goes on. Let there be peace between us, at least, for a while.'

CLAUDIA AND THE MAGIC SHIP

'Oh, cruel, cruel fate! Our gods are punishing us!'

That's what the Romans said when enemies from north Africa surrounded their city, when their crops died in their fields and when famine threatened to kill them all. Even worse, when Roman priests held auguries (rituals) to try to foretell the future, the predictions were always bad. Very bad indeed.

What could the Romans do? Their soldiers fought bravely, but the African army was better. Should they just give up hope, and wait to die?

The Senate (ruling council of Rome) held emergency meetings. 'It would be risky,' said the Senators, 'but dare we consult the Sibyl's books for some advice?'

The Sibyl was a strange and dangerous priestess. Her warnings and prophecies had been collected in books as strange as the Sibyl herself. Their contents could not always be trusted, and were very difficult to understand.

But there was no-one else to ask for advice. So the books were brought out from the temple, and shown to the Senators.

The Sibyl's words were puzzling and surprising: 'Rome will be freed by a mother from overseas.' What did that mean? The Senate decided that the Sibyl wanted them to invite Cybele, a goddess from lands to the east of Rome, to come to live in their city. Cybele was famous as the Great Mother who helped crops grow, and a powerful guardian in times of war.

It was a hot summer day. Crowds of eager Romans shuffled and jostled each other as they waited on the river bank. She was coming! Great Cybele! The goddess who would save their city!

The Senators, priests and respected old citizens stood calm and dignified. They were excited, too, but they would not show it.

Was that her ship there, in the distance? No, just heat haze. But yes! Wait! There was a ship. Cybele had reached Rome. Well, almost...

As the crowds waved and cheered, the ship carrying the statue of the goddess shuddered and came to a sudden stop. The sailors prodded at the river bed with long wooden oars. But the ship stayed stuck, refusing to move.

But who was that, alone, right beside the river? A mature, married woman? Alone in public? The old men and Senators tutted among themselves. That was not respectable. Who was she? Oh, it was Claudia Quinta! She came from a very good family and she should know better. But the Senators had already had to tell her off for speaking out about politics. A decent woman should stay silent in public!

And what was Claudia doing? Three times she bent down, scooped up handfuls of river water and poured it over her head. Three time she raised her hands to the skies. Was the heat making her ill? Was she going mad?

Whatever next!? Now she was kneeling and had untied her long hair so that it fell over her face. See, she was praying.

'Oh Great Mother,' she chanted. (Dear me, what a voice.) 'Help me, please! They say I've brought shame to my family, but I've done nothing wrong.'

'Send me a sign, I beg you, to prove that I'm a good woman. Then I'll say prayers to you for the rest of my life.'

Claudia stood up, and walked towards the ship, which was still stuck in the river. By now, the sailors were throwing ropes overboard, to tie to trees on the bank to keep the ship under control.

Without really thinking, Claudia stretched out her hand to touch a ship's rope, trailing in the water. A strange deep roaring seemed to echo across the river. Or was it just distant thunder?

With a graceful swirl and swoosh, Cybele's magic ship began to move. Claudia picked up the rope and pulled very gently, and the ship followed her.

Slowly, in a daze, Claudia walked along the river bank until she reached the harbour, with the ship gliding smoothly behind her. The crowds cheered and waved, but she hardly saw them. At first, the

Senators were dumbfounded, but then they gave orders for splendid celebrations. The music and dancing, sports and feasting lasted for days.

Thanks to Claudia, Cybele had come to Rome!

GREEDY FOR GOLD

Her story is short, but not sweet. Tarpeia was a traitor.

Tarpeia was a young priestess dedicated to Vesta, the goddess of Roman homes. Every day she led prayers and looked after the holy fire that must never go out in Vesta's temple.

Tarpeia carried out all her duties with care. She always looked calm and serene. But inside, she was very unhappy. She longed to leave the temple, to go out and about in the city and meet other people. Most of all, she wanted to wear nice clothes and jewellery; she was especially fond of wearing gold.

Shut away inside the temple, Tarpeia heard how Rome was being attacked by fierce tribesmen, with strange looks, strange manners and strange clothing. People said that even ordinary soldiers wore massive rings, bracelets and armbands of pure gold. Could that really be true?

Tarpeia could not rest; she wanted to see these strangers. So one day she crept out of the temple and walked down to the city walls.

Pulling her veil over her face, so that guards at the gate would not recognise her, she hid behind a heavy wagon taking rubbish out of the city and hurried over to where a group of enemy tribesmen were standing. They did indeed look strange. Not like Romans at all. And, yes! Their arms really did gleam and glitter with huge, heavy, gold-studded shields and magnificent gold bracelets.

Tarpeia knew that she was doing wrong, but she could not help herself. Unveiling her face and smiling, she pointed first to the tribesmen's arms and then to a very old, very secret opening in the city walls. Known only to a few priests and priestesses, it was almost completely hidden behind thick, thorny bushes.

'Come with me,' she said, smiling and beckoning. 'I'll show you how to get inside the walls of Rome.'

The tribesmen looked at each other, shrugged, smirked, picked up their swords and followed her. Tarpeia led the way. Once again, she pointed to the strangers' gleaming arms and made greedy, grasping signs. 'Give them to me!' she said. 'Give them to me.'

But instead – oh Tarpeia! The strangers didn't hand over their golden bracelets. Oh no, they surrounded her and crushed her to death with their heavy, gold-decorated shields.

Luckily for the Romans, the tribesmen were

unable to invade. Rome's guardian god Janus, who loved peace and protected all ways into the city, made magic jets of boiling water gush all over the invaders. They fled in terror.

THE GEESE
THAT SAVED ROME

Yet again, the Romans were at war. This time, their enemies were invaders from Gaul (now France). The Roman army bravely marched out to meet them, but was overpowered and savagely defeated. Many Roman soldiers died in the fighting; others were cut down by sharp Gaulish swords as they fled in panic from the battlefield; still more drowned as they tried to swim back across the river in their heavy armour. The few survivors who did manage to reach Rome left the city gates open as they rushed to seek shelter with their families.

At first, the Gauls were afraid to enter Rome and take control. They feared a trap. Surely, Roman soldiers would be waiting for them, in hiding? But in fact, the Romans were running scared. Almost every man, woman and child who could manage the climb retreated to the Capitol, a cluster of temples and government buildings atop one of Rome's highest, steepest hills.

After watching and waiting, the Gauls plucked up courage to enter Rome, but they found many streets deserted. The Gauls looted and set fire to as much of Rome as they could reach. From the Capitol, the Romans looked down in horror through clouds of smoke as their homes and workshops burned to ashes. For

the moment they were safe, but already they were running short of food and drinking water. Would it soon be their turn to die?

Nearby cities that were friendly with Rome tried to help. They sent messengers to Rome, offering aid. Secretly, skilfully, they climbed the steep Capitoline Hill to meet with Roman leaders. Together, the Romans and their friends agreed to pay the Gauls a rich ransom to go away: 1,000 pounds (about 2,000 kilograms) of gold.

The Roman leaders scrambled down from the Capitol to meet Brennus, the Gauls' army commander. They put the agreed amount of gold on the scales. But Brennus threw his heavy sword on to his side of the balance, turning it in his favour. When the Romans protested that this was not fair, Brennus retorted in words that have been used by conquerors ever since:

'Vae Victis!' he said, using the Roman language, Latin. Or as we might say today, 'Too bad, losers!'

The Romans had no choice. They went away, to find more gold. Meanwhile, spies from the Gauls' army had been watching the messengers climbing up and down the Capitol hill. They decided to try to follow the same route. That way, they would be able to get inside the very heart of Rome.

It was late at night. Roman soldiers guarding the Capitol paced anxiously to and fro, but it was dark and they could see very little. Their watchdogs dozed, but thankfully the geese that guarded goddess Juno's temple were always alert and on the lookout for danger. The slightest sound disturbed them. Right now they definitely had heard something. A faint footfall, perhaps? A slight snapping of a twig? Whatever it was, the noise they made was loud enough to wake the dead.

The Capitol guards sprang into action. Yes, the geese were right! Look, there were Gaulish warriors, climbing up the steep rocks below. A few well-aimed spears soon got rid of them, and Rome was safe once more.

PAST, PRESENT, FUTURE

The early Romans lived in dangerous times. They faced threats from neighbouring cities, from traitors or rivals within Rome itself, and, or so they believed, from angry gods and evil spirits.

Roman people thought these gods and spirits were everywhere. But they were usually silent and invisible. So how could anyone ask them for advice, or know what they did or did not want their worshippers to do? Roman writers told many stories about ways of communicating with the gods. Here are just three:

THE GOD UNDERGROUND

Long, long ago, a Roman farmer was ploughing his fields. His plough dug deeper than usual, and to his horror, he unearthed a body. But the body was not like any person the farmer had ever seen. It was child-sized and child-shaped. But it had the head of a balding, grey-haired, grey-bearded old man.

Stranger still, the body was not dead, but very much alive. Its eyelids flickered. Its mouth opened. It began to speak to him!

The farmer fled in terror, back to his home and family. Trembling, he went to see the temple priest.

'Ah! You have just met Tages,' replied the priest, nodding wisely. 'He's a very ancient god, belonging to the Etruscans who lived here before we Romans arrived. And they claim he taught them a strange and special skill: how to cut open dead animals and 'read' their guts very carefully. They believe that messages from the gods are hidden there. And Etruscan haruspices (soothsayers) have taught Roman priests how to do this, too.'

BEWARE, BEWARE!

Roman priests and people also looked for divine messages hidden in the flight of birds, or in sudden changes of the weather, or in strange behaviour by animals. It was very dangerous to ignore these!

Mighty army commander Julius Caesar, who led Roman legions to invade Britain, was once warned by a soothsayer not to go and make a speech in Rome's great Forum (open-air meeting place). The soothsayer claimed that the day was doomed. Priests had sacrificed an ox to the gods, cut it open and, weirdly, could not find any heart inside. The ox must have been a monster; only magic could have kept it alive. This, the soothsayer said, was undoubtedly an awful warning from the gods.

Caesar scoffed. He was too important, too powerful, too busy to believe such nonsense. He went to the Forum... and was murdered.

SIBYL AND THE BURNING BOOKS

Oracles were people, usually women – sometimes drugged, sometimes ill, sometimes truly, deeply religious – who believed that gods or spirits spoke through them. They were living links between the everyday world of ordinary humans and the terrifying kingdoms of the heavens above and the underworld below. The most famous Roman oracle was the Sibyl. Her power to see into the future came from Apollo, god of music, learning and the arts. She was wise, and dangerous.

King Tarquin of Rome was nicknamed 'the Proud', because he was. Proud and stubborn. One day, the Sibyl went to see him and offered to sell him nine magic books. They contained all the prophecies she had ever made. They foretold what would happen to Rome in the future.

'Far too expensive. Take them away!' said Tarquin. 'Go back to your cave and stop bothering me!'

The Sibyl went away, but not to her cave. Instead, she lit a bonfire, and burned three of the books.

She went back to Tarquin, and offered him the remaining six books, for the same price as she had originally offered all nine.

'Don't be ridiculous!' said Tarquin. 'I've already said the price was far too high.'

So the Sibyl went away and burned another three books. Now only three survived. She went back to Tarquin again.

'If I burn these last three books, then all my knowledge, all my warnings and all my advice to Rome will be lost for ever,' she said. 'It's your choice. But don't keep me waiting.'

Tarquin, proud though he was, had to give in. He could not risk losing all the Sibyl's wisdom. So he paid the full price for nine books for the remaining three.

The Sibyl vanished into thin air.

In later centuries, the Sibyl's three books became some of Rome's most treasured possessions. Like myths and legends, they survived because they helped Roman people make sense of the uncertain world that they lived in. And they linked Rome's past, present and future.

GLOSSARY

Etruscans
Early people who lived in
central Italy.

Gaul
Roman name for the land that
is now France.

Haruspices
Etruscan soothsayers who
claimed to find messages
from the gods in the bodies
of dead animals.

Hostage
Person taken prisoner and
used to force the hostage's
friends to obey the captors'
demands.

Nymphs
Young female nature-spirits.

Oath
Solemn promise.

Oracle
Person who spoke words
believed to come directly
from the gods.

Prophecies
Forecasts of future events.

Sabines
Early people who lived in Italy
close to where the city
of Rome was built.

Senate
Ruling council of Rome.

Soothsayers
People who claim to foretell
the future.

Truce
Pause in fighting, agreed
between enemies.